story and illustrations by
Mark Summers

E
FRISCH,
AARON

Published in 2012 by Creative Editions
P.O. Box 227, Mankato, MN 56002 USA
Creative Editions is an imprint of The Creative Company.
Designed by Rita Marshall
Printed in Italy
Library of Congress Cataloging-in-Publication Data
Frisch, Aaron.
Pirates at the plate / by Aaron Frisch;
illustrated by Mark Summers.
Summary: Teams of pirates and cowboys, including
such figures as Blackbeard and Wild Bill, inject rowdy
adventure into America's pastime in this story
about baseball and the imagination of youth.
ISBN 978-1-56846-210-3
[1. Baseball—Fiction. 2. Pirates—Fiction. 3. Cowboys—Fiction.
4. Imagination—Fiction.] I. Summers, Mark, ill. II. Title.
PZ7.F9169Pi 2012   [E]—dc23   20011040837

First edition
2 4 6 8 9 7 5 3 1

written by Aaron Frisch

creative & editions

Pirates at the Plate

Welcome to the ballyard, fans. We're in the bottom of the 22nd inning, score knotted at 47 runs apiece, Pirates at the plate.

• •

Wild Bill is on the hill and throwing heat for the Cowboys. And folks, they don't call him "Wild" for nothing.

Good thing the Cowboys have Hopalong Cassidy warming up in the bullpen.

Long John Silver digs into the box. Nobody out, and Calico Jack is aboard second base. This is a dangerous at bat for the Cowboys …

… because the Pirates have the big-bopping Blackbeard waiting on deck.

pp

There's the windup … and the pitch … and Long John blasts one deep to center field!

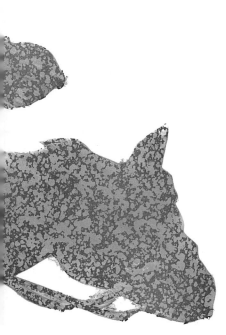

The Cisco Kid's gonna have to giddy-up if he wants to catch this ball!

15

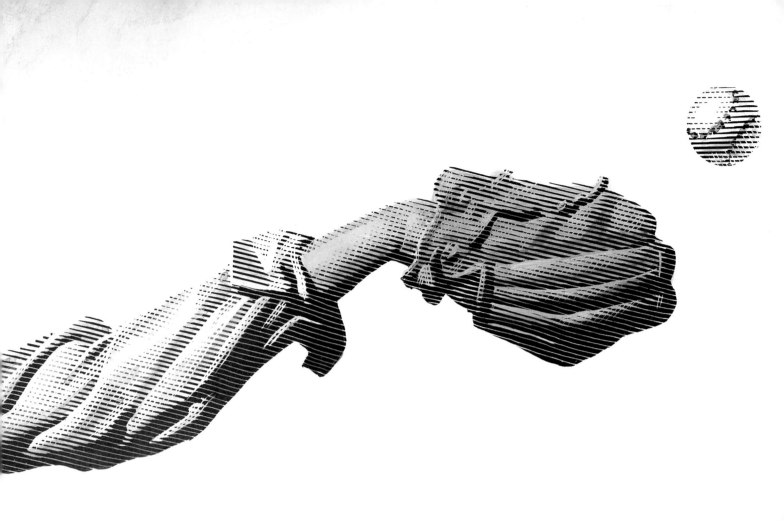

Way, way back he goes … and makes
a spectacular grab at the warning track!

The Kid slings the ball to the infield, and now Calico Jack's in a real pickle, as the Cowboys have him caught in a rundown.

But hold on—what's this? Long John is trying to steal second base! In fact, he's already heaved first base into his loot sack.

20

The umpire is going to halt the action here. He's told both teams before no weapons, ropes, or shovels.

Captain Hook doesn't like that ruling at all, and here he comes out of the Pirates' dugout. It looks like the Cowboys' manager, Bat Masterson, has a beef, too.

"I'm tellin' ya for the last time, ya lily-livered seadog," Masterson says. "Quit rustlin' the dern bases, or we'll toss the lot of ya in the hoosegow."

"Who ye be callin' lily-livered, ye bow-legged landlubber?" Hook says. "Yer boys play like Barbies."

"Is zat so?"   "Yarr!"

Uh-oh. Here we go again. The benches are clearing, and this could be the messiest dustup yet. Long John is unscrewing his peg leg and—

"Stewart!

Dinner!"

"But Mom, the guys are just about to …! Oh, all right. I'm coming."

How 'bout that. Another game called on account of spaghetti.

$\mathcal{B}$oth teams hit the lockers. I guess this one's going down as a tie.

Join us again tomorrow, fans, for another humdinger of a matchup …

. . . .

… as the always feisty Vikings clash with the undefeated Tigers.